The Nutcracker Ballet

RETOLD BY MELISSA HAYDEN

ILLUSTRATIONS BY STEPHEN T. JOHNSON

A Donna Martin Book

Andrews and McMeel · Kansas City

Library of Congress Cataloging-in-Publication Data

Hayden, Melissa.
   The Nutcracker ballet / retold by Melissa Hayden ; illustrations by Stephen T. Johnson.
      p.   cm.
   "A Donna Martin book."
   Summary: Relates the story of the popular ballet, in which a little girl travels with the
Nutcracker Prince to the Land of Sweets.
   ISBN 0-8362-4501-6
   1. Nutcracker (Ballet)—Juvenile literature. [1. Nutcracker (Ballet) 2. Ballets—Stories,
plots, etc.] I. Johnson, Stephen, 1964– ill. II. Title.
GV1790.N8H39 1992
792.8'4—dc20   92-20654
                                                                      CIP
                                                                      AC

Book design and calligraphy by Rick Cusick
Typeset by Connell-Zeko
Printed by Tien Wah Press

PREFACE

The Nutcracker story has a very long history, beginning with a tale written by a German, E.T.A. Hoffmann, in 1816, called The Nutcracker and the Mouse King. *This story, which has been widely translated into English and retold in children's storybooks, is a considerably darker story of black magic and evil than the joyous ballet by the same name.*

The ballet came circuitously by way of France and Russia to the United States, where it has become an annual event heralding Christmas across the land. When the great Russian composer Tchaikovsky worked on a ballet to the Nutcracker story together with a Frenchman named Marius Petipa, Petipa selected a considerably gentler French adaptation of the Hoffmann story called The Nutcracker of Nuremburg *by Alexandre Dumas, père (meaning father, because his son was also a writer). Although Petipa was to be the choreographer (the person who planned the dance steps), he fell ill before the rehearsals and the dance movements to the finished music and plot were assigned to a man named Lev Ivanov.*

The first performance took place in St. Petersburg, Russia, on December 18, 1892. While the music for Tchaikovsky's ballet is considered among his finest compositions, very little of the choreography has survived from the original production.

The first complete production of The Nutcracker Ballet *in the United States was choreographed by William Christensen for the San Francisco Ballet in 1944. Then an important figure in the history of dance, George Balanchine, choreographer of the New York City Ballet, staged his production in 1954. Balanchine, who was Russian-born, had an intimate acquaintance with* The Nutcracker Ballet. *In 1919, at the age of 15, Balanchine danced the role of the Nutcracker in the very theater in which it was originally performed.*

Balanchine's choreography, which has had numerous adaptations, forms the basis for most of the productions seen today. Many of Balanchine's own principal dancers are associated with ballet troupes scattered across the country. As millions of people watch the lovely story of how Clara (sometimes Marie) saved the life of the Nutcracker and restored the Nutcracker Prince to his Land of Sweets, they may take pleasure in knowing that a tradition begun in 1892 in St. Petersburg continues unbroken.

—M.H.

Is THERE ANY DAY MORE EXCITING THAN CHRISTMAS EVE? Any day more full of secret errands, whispered preparations, mysterious boxes, and dreamy visions? Certainly not for Clara. Today was Christmas Eve, and tonight her family would give their annual Christmas Eve party. All her uncles and aunts and cousins, friends and neighbors—even her grandparents—would gather at her house to admire the Christmas tree the grownups had decorated to surprise the children. They would exchange gifts, they would dance and be merry, and Clara and her brother Fritz would be allowed to stay up way past their bedtimes.

Just this afternoon as Clara served her dolls tea in the playroom off the parlor, she could hardly suppress her curiosity as she spoke to Fritz about the evening's festivities. "I wonder what Herr Drosselmeyer will do tonight to entertain the children?" She might have been a little afraid of this strange man with his fearsome cape and wild gray hair and menacing eye patch if he were not such a good family friend. Her parents had even made him her godfather. "And I wonder what he will bring me?" she added.

At this, Fritz, who had been lining up his toy soldiers in regimental order, cried out mischievously, "Watch out for your tea party!" Commanding two of his soldiers to fire their toy cannon he lobbed a peppermint right over to the dolls, just missing a china teacup.

———

"Children," called their mother, "it is time to dress!" And as the maid whisked them out of the playroom, Clara carefully laid down her favorite doll—a gift of Herr Drosselmeyer—for a nap on its doll bed. When they came down for the party, she knew, soldiers and dolls would be neatly reassembled near the tree, peacefully coexisting in the spirit of Christmas.

Dressed now in the pretty new frock her mother had bought her for the party, Clara could no longer contain her curiosity. A peek through the keyhole into the parlor gave her a tantalizing glimpse of the bustling activity within, but the pesky Fritz soon shoved her aside. She could only wait and listen for the magic moment when the first guest arrived and she and Fritz would be allowed to enter the parlor.

Outside, in the crisp winter night, she knew, the chestnut man would be tempting passersby with his steaming treats. Clara thought she heard a jumble of voices that might be the guests as they strolled toward the gate. Was a child asking for some of the warm roasted chestnuts? Or perhaps those were the voices of children excitedly examining the toy seller's wares. Herr Drosselmeyer, she was sure, would be coming with his gifts.

At last! Clara and Fritz were allowed to go into the parlor! The tree was beautiful, decorated with candles and ornaments and confections of every description. And nearby were her dolls and their furniture and Fritz's soldiers standing at attention without Fritz to distract them.

As the guests arrived, they handed their coats and hats to the maid, then came forward to greet Clara's parents and to admire the tree. And at last Herr Drosselmeyer arrived, causing a great stir. Dressed in his cape he looked so mysterious that Clara hung back—until he flung it open theatrically and drew her into his arms. Behind him was a boy so laden with gifts she could barely see him.

After directing the boy to lay down the gifts, Herr Drosselmeyer introduced him with a flourish. "This is my nephew," he said—but he did not give his name. Clara thought he was handsome, and she wondered why she had never seen him before.

Herr Drosselmeyer was known as an inventor of mechanical things who had a talent for repairing clocks. Upon glancing at the grandfather clock in the parlor with the carved owl atop it, he pronounced that it was not keeping time properly. Consulting his own pocket watch, he corrected the time, fixing the clock so quickly his actions seemed like magic.

Then with a sweep of his cape he drew attention to the two huge boxes he had brought into the parlor. As he opened them one by one, out came two life-size mechanical dolls. Winding up the first, a ballerina, he set her to doing a beautiful dance until, like a music box, she slowly wound down and came to a stop. He put her away and brought out the second, a soldier. Standing straight and tall, the soldier performed with great dignity and precision until he too wound down and was retired to his box.

Oh, how wonderful these toys were! thought Clara. Were they her present? No, said her mother, they were for all the children—just a special entertainment for the evening, like the colored scarves Herr Drosselmeyer often magically pulled out of nowhere to the delight of onlookers.

But now Herr Drosselmeyer brought forth yet another surprise—a little wooden man with an ugly face, broad jaws, a white beard and white hair. He was dressed like a soldier. What a quaint little fellow, thought Clara. What could he be?

Then Herr Drosselmeyer and his nephew produced some nuts and her godfather demonstrated the wonderful power of the little wooden man. Placing a nut between the Nutcracker's broad jaws, Herr Drosselmeyer pulled down at the wooden coattails and the nutshell was cracked, revealing a perfect, unbroken nutmeat. When Herr Drosselmeyer presented it to Clara, all of the children clamored for nuts of their own. One by one, Herr Drosselmeyer fed the nuts to the Nutcracker and placed a perfect nutmeat into each out-reached hand. Then he turned with a bow to Clara. "This is my present to you," he said.

So the Nutcracker was her gift. What a wonderful present! Clara embraced the Nutcracker as the children drew 'round to admire him. Suddenly, naughty Fritz, in a fit of jealousy, grabbed the Nutcracker, jostled his way through the children, threw the Nutcracker to the floor, and stepped on him.

How sad Clara was. She picked up the Nutcracker and examined him. His powerful jaws could no longer close hard upon the nuts. Herr Drosselmeyer came to comfort her, wrapping his handkerchief around the Nutcracker's jaw like a sling on a soldier wounded in battle.

———————

Clara loved the Nutcracker no less for his misfortune and cradled him in her arms. The other little girls gathered 'round and they too cradled dolls and began to sing lullabies to them.

But the naughty boys—all as full of mischief as Fritz—were gathering forces to disrupt the peaceful lullabies of the girls. With noisy bugles they marched right into the center of the makeshift nursery and sent the girls scurrying. Ignoring them as best they could, the girls assembled once again—but the boys marched in again!

Enough! The fathers grabbed the boys and some got a good paddling! It was time for more sociable behavior from these young men. As the parents organized the children for a dance, Herr Drosselmeyer's handsome nephew came forth to give Clara a doll bed for the injured Nutcracker.

In the merriment of dancing, the boys' misbehavior was forgotten. Parents and children danced together and even Clara's grandparents joined in at the end. At last the children grew tired and it was time for all the guests to go home. Gathering their coats and hats, lifting the little ones to their shoulders, the fathers and mothers said their good nights to their hosts. Last to leave were Herr Drosselmeyer and his nephew. What a nice boy he was, Clara thought again as they departed.

"Up now to bed, children," said Mother, and Clara and Fritz obeyed, knowing that Christmas Day would soon be upon them.

As she undressed, Clara thought of her Nutcracker lying on the doll bed under the tree. Just one more look at her precious new Nutcracker, she thought, just to be sure he was all right.

In her gown she crept down to the parlor. How beautiful the tree was! And there was her Nutcracker safe and sound, with Herr Drosselmeyer's handkerchief wrapped around his injured jaw. She picked him up and, thinking dreamily of the magic of Christmas and her mysterious benefactor, Herr Drosselmeyer, she lay down on the couch with the Nutcracker nestled in her arms. Soon she was fast asleep.

Was everyone in bed, Mother wondered? Taking up her candle she tiptoed down the hall to find Fritz sound asleep. But where was Clara? She descended the staircase and found Clara on the couch, her Nutcracker clasped in her arms. By the soft smile on her face, Mother knew Clara had fallen asleep and was probably dreaming. Rather than wake her, she covered Clara with her shawl and left her to her pleasant dreams.

But no sooner had Mother returned upstairs than Herr Drosselmeyer reappeared from out of the darkness! Tiptoeing toward her, he gently pried the Nutcracker from Clara's arms, removed his handkerchief, and instantly repaired him. He put the Nutcracker back into Clara's arms without disturbing her.

But what was this? Suddenly Clara fluttered awake to the most remarkable sights and sounds! Wasn't that Herr Drosselmeyer standing above the owl on the grandfather clock waving his arms as the clock struck midnight? Clara rose and put the Nutcracker back on his bed.

Then something extraordinary happened. Before her very eyes the Christmas tree appeared to grow to an enormous height. Meanwhile, Clara saw that she herself was no larger than Fritz's soldiers, who were now standing at the ready under the tree. And there was Herr Drosselmeyer again, flapping his cape in the corner. Suddenly, some mice quite as big as Clara came scampering toward the tree, as if Herr Drosselmeyer had ushered them in. Were they after the sweets on the tree? Why would Herr Drosselmeyer let them in?

She turned to look for the Nutcracker and found him lying on his bed, but the bed seemed to be as big as the one in her own bedroom, and the Nutcracker lay on it like a full-size soldier!

As the mice entered, the soldiers came out from under the tree to face them. Now Clara feared a full-scale battle was beginning, with Herr Drosselmeyer nowhere in sight. Even the sentries left their sentry posts to form flanks against the attack. The mice came in wave after wave and seemed to overwhelm the soldiers. The soldiers rolled out their cannon and fired repeatedly at their attackers. But they seemed to be losing as the fearsome Mouse King, his crown upon his head, came forward to survey the battle.

Clara rushed to rouse the Nutcracker. "Quick!" she cried. "The soldiers cannot defend the tree! Without your help, the mice will eat all the sweets on it!" So the Nutcracker rose from his bed to do battle with the Mouse King. The Mouse King was a menacing creature and caught every thrust of the Nutcracker's sword with his own, finally forcing the Nutcracker backward. Though he valiantly sought to drive his sword through the Mouse King, the Nutcracker fell down!

———

The Mouse King advanced, confident of landing the telling blow. Without thinking twice, Clara took her slipper and threw it at the Mouse King. Distracted, he looked backward, giving the Nutcracker just enough time to rise and move decisively to stab the Mouse King. After falling heavily, the Mouse King writhed and twitched, then lay dead. Triumphant, the Nutcracker removed the slain Mouse King's crown with his sword, and took it to place on Clara's head. But poor Clara had fainted onto the bed.

Solemnly, the Nutcracker, whose life had been saved by Clara, placed the crown on her head, just as he might crown a princess. Then a strange and beautiful thing happened as Clara lay in a faint on the bed. The bed spun its way through the starry night, accompanied by the Nutcracker.

And then—though Clara was still in a faint and did not see it—the Nutcracker, shedding his homely wooden face and broad jaw and white whiskers, revealed himself to be a prince!

When Clara awoke, she found herself in a winter wonderland with a handsome prince—a prince who looked exactly like Herr Drosselmeyer's nephew—beside her.

"Thanks to you," said the Nutcracker Prince, "I can finally go back to my home in the Land of Sweets."

"I don't understand," said Clara.

"Where I come from, in the Land of Sweets, the Mouse Queen had cast a spell on a princess, making her ugly," he explained. "With the help of my uncle, Herr Drosselmeyer, the royal clock-maker, I cracked a very hard nut with my jaws. This broke the spell, restoring her beauty, and as a reward, I was made a prince myself. But in turn I was put under a spell by the Mouse Queen, doomed to be a wooden nutcracker. Because I was under a spell and had become so ugly, my uncle and I were driven out of the Land of Sweets."

Suddenly Clara understood that Herr Drosselmeyer had a purpose in all the strange things he had done that night. He had brought her the Nutcracker and set up the decisive battle in her very own parlor!

"Because you helped me to destroy the Mouse King and his army, I am restored to a prince and can return to my homeland," the Nutcracker Prince said. "If the mice had been victorious, they might have gone on to eat all the sweets in my land. Come with me and you will see the most wonderful things you have ever seen."

"But I must be back on Christmas morning or Mother will miss me!" said Clara.

"Indeed you shall be," he said.

As they began walking, it started to snow heavily and soon the snow danced around them. Then the Nutcracker Prince led Clara to a little boat made of the magical nutshell he had split to liberate the princess in the Land of Sweets.

"This will take us to my beautiful country," he said, and they sailed down a river of chocolate sauce to the place he called home.

It was, as the Nutcracker Prince had said, an extraordinary place. Candy canes grew like trees. Strawberry ice cream cones as big as a house glistened in the shimmering light. The Sugar Plum Fairy and her cavalier welcomed them.

"We have missed you," she said to the Nutcracker Prince. "Tell us your adventures."

The Nutcracker told them of the whole dangerous battle, how the mice stormed the toy soldiers, how they lay near defeat, how the Mouse King arrived ready to declare victory, how Clara roused him to battle, how the Mouse King almost killed him as he fell backward, how Clara bravely flung her slipper at the Mouse King, distracting him, and in doing so had saved the Nutcracker Prince's life.

"What a brave girl you are!" said the Sugar Plum Fairy. "As your reward you shall see the most wonderful sweets and treats in our kingdom." And saying that, she led Clara and the Nutcracker Prince to a throne, where they would watch the most gala performance ever assembled in the Land of Sweets.

Spanish hot chocolate swirled grandly, with the heat and passion of its native land.

Arabian coffee floated through, its seductive aroma lingering.

Tea from China popped comically from its box and bubbled with glee.

Russian treats danced with the fervor of Cossack soldiers.

Mother Ginger smirked and primped, suddenly revealing a host of tiny creatures hiding in her skirts.

"And now, my cavalier and I will dance in your honor," said the Sugar Plum Fairy. It was the most beautiful dance Clara had ever seen.

"I must take Clara back to her home now," said the Nutcracker Prince.

"Ah, yes, your carriage awaits you," said the Sugar Plum Fairy. Then she took Clara's hand. "Sometimes it takes great courage to defend something ugly or injured," she said. "But you have learned that wonderful things can happen to children who take such risks."

In moments, Clara and the Nutcracker Prince were seated in a wondrous sleigh. The Sugar Plum Fairy and her cavalier and all the sweets and treats who had entertained them waved goodbye as they crossed through the sky. Soon Clara would find herself snug at home, awakening to the beauty of Christmas Day.

———